Quantum Entanglement

Unforsaken Grimm

Volume 8

Ralph K Jones

RALPH JONES

First edition October 2019

Book design and Illustration Daria Popkova

Book and concept Illustrator, based in Kharkiv, Ukraine.

www.ralphkjones.com

Disclaimer: This fictional work lives as much as you do. It conveys an intriguing story that stands the test of time, but, like yourself, it is merely the work of an author's imagination. It breathes, cries, and yearns to be solid, but it remains tethered to the realm of fiction. All three of us--the author, the reader, and the book--can claim to be no realer than the other. If you are reading this, then know that any similarities to real places, people, or events, are just a coincidence. But if that's the case, then we are not real either.

Table of Contents

Hierarchy of Monsters

Hierarchy of Monsters

From deep under the grass, deep under the dirt, even deep under the very stone, he stirred. Alan sat up slowly and stretched his long thick green arms. He groaned loudly in a deep monotone as he shook out his stiff and rotting limbs.

Around him, several other zombies started to do the same. It was getting close to twilight; everyone could feel it. Alan shuffled through the rough-cut corridors of the stone cave followed by his green and grumpy brothers. Though it was cold and dark, with only the light from some lava vents lighting up the chamber, it was a place they all thought of as home.

Alan entered a large room where various under-dwellers milled; zombies, skeletons, spiders, and demons, all getting ready to go to work on the ground above. Around were piles of jagged body parts, weapons, and various other tools of the trade. The siege of the lands above was serious business and it never was good to go up unprepared.

A tall spectre moved to a stone podium, catching the attention of all gathered.

"Right!" the spectre began eagerly. "Just wanted to thank everyone for coming out this evening and before we all head out just wanted to go over a few things. As you all know we have had great success in human hunting lately. There has been a decent kill count, BUT! I notice a lot of structures are left standing. Killing humans is not enough when we leave their resources laying around.

Soon the group was dismissed, and Alan met up with Fred, a skeleton he fought with many times. As the pair walked, the light began to peer into the tunnel from ahead, the tell-tale blue of the night could be seen, and the sounds of spiders and other denizens of the darkness could be heard already working beyond. At the exit stood a single skeleton, he held a series of wood blocks with writing on them.

"Got a moment to talk about the players?" the skeleton asked in a polite tone.

"Players?" Alan asked, confused. "What are those?"

"Religious malarkey," Fred responded dismissively. "Some seem to believe in some kind of external force controlling our destiny."

"It is true!" the skeleton insisted. "The players enabled our world and come here to create! We are but slaves to the will of their higher power."

"No player controls me," Fred responded in an annoyed tone. "I wander where I like and bite who I like."

"The humans serve the players!" the skeleton added. "They guide them to create our world as they see fit, they are geniuses who shape all that there is."

Alan shook his head as he joined his friend out into the forest biome land beyond. Players or not this was a strange wonderful world that did not always make sense to the young zombie.

"Well, I think this is where we part ways for the night," Fred said as he looked around. "I'm going to go this way and see if I can find some humans looking for food."

"That's fine," Alan nodded as he looked toward a section of trees. "I'm going to try this way. I got a feeling there might be something good through the forest."

Before long, Alan's tenacity paid off as a small house came into view just over a tall hill. The house was mostly made of wood with a short roof and chimney. Parts of the building looked to have been replaced by stone and as he moved to look Alan noticed the back of the house was missing altogether.

A sudden movement caused Alan to pause, going silent to avoid notice as a figure emerged from inside the house and began to work on the hole with tools. He crept forward, raising his arms as if to bite. The human at the last second turned, spotting Alan and drawing a sword. Alan tried to flee but a second human came out and slew him before he could even mount a defence.

"Damn those things are stupid," one of the humans commented. "They got slower since the last patch."

"Yeah, they nerfed them because the lowbies kept whining about dying."

"This game is lame anyway," the first human replied. "I heard there was a new game where you literally dive in and feel the adventure."

"Isn't that the one where the girl went into the coma?" the second human asked.

"Yeah but that was the beta," the first human replied. "I am sure they have it fixed by now.

Laid in Waiting

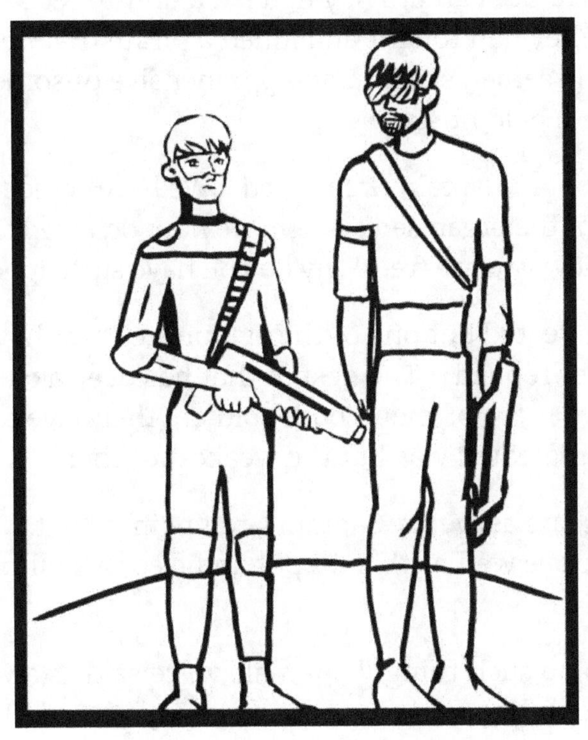

Laid in Waiting

Captain Grell and Striker moved forward but the colonists still seemed to be scared. They had led a unit to recover the far-off colony. They had fought and killed a pirate that held them, but they still seemed scared and apprehensive of something as if they still were held hostage.

"What is wrong?" Captain Grell asked. "We have come from the central hub of the organised system, we have defeated the space pirate, and now you are free. Why do you have such apprehension?"

"You have defeated but one of the evil pirates that have enslaved us," a villager replied. "The despot that has overtaken these lands has two more of them, both soldiers that have taken us. The one you defeated was but the weakest of them."

"We are soldiers as well," Captain Grell pointed out. "We will take them out as well as this despot and free this outpost and planet."

"You will do no such thing," a female voice said as a woman walked in from deep within the colony. "My name is Tai, and I am a saboteur. I have tainted the water and crops and if I am not appeased, I will not tell anyone how to circumvent it. Soon will be famine and then death."

"My name is Arina," another woman said as she walked closer. "I know that there are few soldiers here, so I have allied with the local pirates in the system and promised them riches if they invaded. All it would take would be a message from me and this colony would be overrun."

A large man came out of one of the buildings. He was massive and commanding, wearing full tactical armour and with a huge blaster on his back. "I am Corren. I know who you are, and you will succeed no further."

"What do you mean?" Captain Grell asked. "My organisation is no secret."

"Not you, silly soldier," Corren scoffed as he pointed to Striker. "You may be poised as a simple mercenary, but you are a great hero known in fourteen sectors. You are the bane of the syndicate master and seem to think you can do as you will out here."

"Well, I suppose the outer systems aren't far enough to outrun my reputation," Striker replied with a grin. "So, what is your plan here? Do you work for the syndicate master?"

"Consider me a private contractor," Corren replied smugly, "I intend to bring this planet to its knees, then the next, then the next. You may have slain my pirate, but I still have much that I can do."

"You are a fool if you think the syndicate master will share power with you," Striker commented with a laugh. "This is a person that has gone from colony to colony, planet to planet, taken everything he wanted, and destroyed the rest. He would say anything to you that he thinks would get you to do anything. These small planets are beneath his notice up until now and as soon as you get them and present them to him, he will snatch them out of your hands and leave you with nothing."

"You would say anything to save your skin," Corren snorted. "I have the people here in the thrall of my fear and my two mercenaries serve me because of my strength."

"Then I will challenge it," Striker replied. "We shall see who is stronger."

"So be it," Corren replied. "There is an old fighting pitch here, one that the colony sometimes used for sport and to decide things that only force, and combat could decide. Fight me and we will see who deserves to decide the fate of this place."

"Let's do it," Striker replied with a grin. "That blaster looks quite formidable. But it does have one flaw."

"And what would that be?" Corren asked.

"It takes too long to draw," Striker said as he drew his pistol and shot Corren in the head.

As he fell, Striker walked forward to the remaining mercenaries. "So, who do you work for now?"

"You!" Both of them said in unison, shocked by what they had just seen.

"Good," Striker replied. "Now get to work and undo what you have done…I got three more despots to take out before I head back to more civilised space."

Building Blocks

Building Blocks

Rei celebrated her victory, knowing that there would be a large cut coming her way. She did not know what gave her the speed and strength she had. She felt like a freak when she was younger, but her mother always told her that she was special. Well, that was when her mother was around. She was stronger than most and healed fast, that was why she fought, that was why she won.

"You know I might know something that might interest you," a man said as he walked up to Rei.

"If it is another fight you will have to wait," Rei replied. "I can't do them back to back.

"It is not like that," the man told her. "It is some news about your mother."

"What do you know about my mother?" Rei asked suspiciously.

"I know far less than I would like," The man commented, "My name is Dresden, I am a…researcher in a similar field of your mother's."

"And what field is that?" Rei asked.

"Genetic engineering," "Dresden replied enthusiastically. "This is a field that right now is booming. We live in a dying world where the side effects of what we are doing are coming back to us. We are becoming immune to drugs, diseases are becoming stronger, and it seems that we are soon to be unfit to live in the world we are making for ourselves."

"I fail to see what this has to do with me," Rei commented flippantly. "I am just a weird girl who is really good at kicking the asses of people bigger than me."

"Well, it has to do with your mother mostly," Dresden replied. "For she has found the cure."

"The cure to what?" Rei asked with a confused look on her face.

"The stagnation of the human genome," Dresden explained. "She is a cross between a mad scientist and a pioneer. Her forward thinking has made it possible that we might have some way to unlock our true potential. Did you know there is a plant in the rainforest that evolved itself to—"

"Let me stop you right there," Rei cut him off. "I knew my mother was into some freaky experiments. I figure she is the direct reason I am as messed up as I am…I am like a beast person…well, part of one."

"You are nearly perfect," Dresden gushed. "And possibly having the potential of full perfection."

Rei sighed. "How about we get to this…how about you tell me what you want."

"I want a genetic sample," Dresden replied. "I have studied much on what she has done and want to see a live sample of her work."

Rei gestured to the blood on the battlefield. "There's some."

"That is tainted and non-viable," Dresden replied as he withdrew a syringe, still in its sterile wrapping. "We would need something much fresher. I guarantee it will be worth your while."

"And what is it that you would offer me?" Rei asked. "I live under the radar and do very well for myself with my talents, such as they are."

"What if I told you that your mother had a secret lab?" Dresden asked conspiratorially, "On that no one other than myself had found? I could tell you where it was."

"What would still be there that you have not already taken?" Rei asked sceptically. "I am a genetic anomaly, not a scientist. There is little that I could do for myself with her tools."

"We have found much there," Dresden told her. "But I think there are still answers there; one's for you and you alone."

"Fine," Rei said as she rolled up her sleeve. "Take it and tell me where it is."

Dresden nodded and took the sample. "It is in the old hospital of your hometown, hidden in the cafeteria."

"I will go then," Rei said as she rolled down her sleeve and walked away. "Good luck with...well whatever."

Dresden smiled as she walked away. "Oh, I will. You have no idea the potential of the genes hidden in your blood."

The Cold Ship

The Cold Ship

L iam arrived on the bridge and looked around to the others on the bridge. "What is going on?"

"We have received a signal," Peters replied. "We think it's a distress call."

"Think?" Liam asked within curiosity. "Aren't distress signals usually pretty cut and dried?"

"We are barely receiving the signal at all," Sam added. "It seems to be coming from a debris field and it is getting cut off. However, the frequency and the recycling seem to mean distress signal. It is definitely too weak to reach deep space rescue and I was considering diverting course to check it out but wanted a second opinion."

"We are going to help, right?" Peters asked. "Is it not the duty of space vessels to respond to distress calls of other vessels. We might be the only hope of this crippled ship for survival."

"Duty...perhaps," Sam mused. "But in no way a regulation. It is ultimately up to the command of the ship to determine if it is safe to proceed. We must weigh this ship and crew against those in need. I will leave this to a vote. This is both dangerous and risks our mission. There is a very high bandit risk out here and we have no way of knowing if this is not an elaborate trap."

"They might have families," Peters added. "Is it not worth the risk to help them? My vote is to assist.

Sam turned to Liam. "Looks like you are the deciding vote. I will do what the consensus desires."

Liam took a deep breath. "Given their location and distance from deep space rescue it would put their chances of survival at twenty-two per cent should we not help. I think that is worth the risk."

"Then it is decided." Sam nodded.

A few moments later the ship slowed to make its careful approach and incursion into the debris field. As anticipated massive stones of rock and metals floated precariously around, threatening to crush smaller vessels into scrap.

"Peters, are you picking up anything from the ship?" Liam asked. "It looks dead in the water to me with no power."

"I am getting no signals from the ship," Peters replied. "No power, no life signs, nothing."

"Can it be part of the debris field?" Sam asked. "Could we just not be able to get any signal?"

"The signals are getting interference, but we should be getting something," Peters explained. "There seems to be legitimately no power coming from the vessel at all."

"Are we too late?" Sam asked. "Did their systems fail?"

"Do a hull temperature reading," Liam suggested. "Even if their power has gone out the air inside should still be running close to internal ambient."

"It's cold," Peters replied. "As cold as the rocks."

"We are about to be attacked!" Liam said urgently. "This is a decoy vessel and the signal must have come from another ship."

"Bring us about!" Sam ordered. "Get us out of here!"

As Liam manipulated the controls and the ship began to turn, two vessels emerged from deep in the debris field and began to close in on the ship.

"Two unidentified craft," Peters informed them. "They are powering up their weapons."

"Evasive action!" Sam commanded, opening up the weapon controls on his panel and bringing them to bear. "I will buy us as much time as we can, continue the retreat. I can't pinpoint the shots. The targeting computers aren't shooting straight!"

"Malfunctions from the other gunners, sir!" Peters confirmed. "No one can get a clear shot!"

The ship was rocked from a torpedo hit, causing the bridge to shake and warning lights to come to life one after another.

"They can hit us!" Sam noted with confusion. "How can they fire so accurately in here?"

"They had time to compensate their equipment," Peters offered. "They probably have this all figured out."

"Tell all weapons masters to use line of sight telemetry," Sam ordered. "Use math if you have to. We need to get some damage on them."

Another explosion shook the ship, a second torpedo slamming the hull. The control panel in front of Liam went red and the ship began violently lurching. In seconds another crash shook the ship, this one not like the torpedo and nearly toppling the bridge crew from their seats.

"Report!" Sam demanded, fighting with his controls that seemed unresponsive.

"The last torpedo knocked us into the debris field," Peters responded. "Massive damage, we are venting atmosphere. Damage reports flooding in throughout the ship."

"Liam?" Sam said as he turned around. "Give me some good news."

"The engines are down," Liam responded. "The hit tore open the drives and we're venting fuel. We're dead in the water."

Sam looked down at his console as if confirming the gravity of the situation. Liam knew that Sam was never one for rash decisions and could see the one forming on his face might be the hardest one that he ever had to make. He took a deep breath and hit all quarters emergency intercom.

"We have to abandon. Signal all hands...we have to abandon ship...I repeat all hands abandon ship!"

Words on the Technical Wind

Words on the Technical Wind

Dealer returned home to his apartment. It was nothing fancy, in fact a place that few could find themselves proud of. He got to his door, checked his camera to make sure it was on and put his magnetic key in the lock. Though on the outside it was a simple door, inside it was his temple. He unlocked the deceptively hidden security door and stepped in.

Though his apartment had a bed, a stove and a dresser, almost all the space was left to computer equipment and tools. The way he found what he found was by being the best at what he did. Technology was a wonder of the modern world and people liked to hide their dirty laundry in it, assuming if they did it better than anyone else it could not be found. Assuming no one knew how to do what he did was how he operated, the one you least expected was potentially the most dangerous.

Dealer sat at his computer looking up newsfeeds, police reports, corporate tickers, anything that might offer him an idea for a story or project. However, frustratingly, as much as he looked there seemed nothing to be found. He was just about to give up when a voice chat window popped up.

"You their dealer?" a voice asked. "I think I might have something for you."

"Boy am I glad to hear from you," Dealer replied jovially. "It seems like a big day on lies and a low one on substance out there. What do you have for me, Scout?"

"Perhaps nothing," Scout replied uncertainly. "But perhaps something big, very big."

"Okay, lay it on me," Dealer said with a nod. "You have my undivided attention."

"Alright," Scout agreed. "It goes like this. I have eyewitness reports and medical reports of a myriad of scientists, geniuses, and scholars all being admitted to hospitals after falling into comas. Medically they appear fine and as of yet there is no explanation as to their conditions. Normally, this would be only a minor curiosity, however they all seem connected and all seem to have the same criteria for their condition. It is far too convenient."

"Few things in this world are convenient by accident," Dealer added. "What is the common thread?"

"They all worked on, or did work for, a brain hub," Scout informed him. "Within the last six months."

"Brain hub?" Dealer inquired with a perked eyebrow. "Like the cloud service thing? Wasn't there like some big health risks put forth with it and causing it to lose popularity and overall consumer confidence?"

"That was a glorified video game chat," Scout replied dismissively. "This is a massive compendium and think tank for next level research; stuff so advanced spies are not even sure what they want to take from it."

Is this a private service?" Dealer asked. "If there are only high-end people using it, there should be no problem predicting who might be affected next."

"It is public, very public," Scout clarified. "There are scientists and scholars from all over connected to this thing as well as civilian geniuses and creative minds. There are literally thousands of people using this. The families of those affected have come to us in the government to look into it. However, the core company, Brain Tech, has mostly buried it with assurances that the people affected had pre-existing health conditions and no link could be found. We did an inquiry but as I said, there seems to be nothing really wrong with them. My office seems convinced that it is just a coincidence and is not going to pursue it."

"Well, I suppose that is what I am here for," Dealer replied. "To look into the things that no one else seems able to or wants to."

"Good luck," Scout replied. "Don't end up in a coma."

"I suppose that would prove I am not as good as I think I am." Dealer laughed. "And if so...I deserve it."

The Dangers
of Progression

The Dangers of Progression

Caren did not know what had happened, she did not know what she did to raise the ire of the people after her. She had just signed up for some medical testing for some extra money, and now she was being chased by what looked like mercenaries. She was on the run, she could not go home, and she could not hide.

A van screeched up beside her, Caren was sure this was the end but a young woman her age poked her head out.

"This is going to seem weird, but I am here to protect you from the people after you," the woman said.

"Well under the circumstances I am all for it," Caren admitted as she let the woman help her into the van.

The vehicle tore off, a masked man at the wheel.

"Don't worry about him," the woman said when she noticed Caren's apprehension. "You can call me Jane...I am someone like you...that has been experimented on."

"I am Caren," Caren replied. "I just thought I was testing some new drugs...I didn't know that I was being targeted."

"You were not just chosen because you volunteered," Jane explained. "You were targeted and that was the way to get closer to you. This is going to sound really farfetched, but the people in charge...people we are not so sure of yet have been doing things to people like you... and me. They wanted to see what you could do, what you could become. That is why they tested you, and that is why they are after you now."

Jane laid Carne down on a cot in the back of the van and began to administer injections. Caren tried to protest. "Wait what is that?"

"They can track you with what they did to you," Jane explained. "I am going to counteract it."

"You are not going to reverse the effects though, right?" Caren asked. "I have never felt better since the procedure.

"That is not something they gave you," Jane responded. "It is something they awakened within you."

"Okay," Caren replied placidly. "Do what you have to do?"

Jane worked away using medical tools. Immediately Caren felt better; her strength not fading.

"I have something in me as well," Jane admitted. "The best way to figure it out is that they wanted something that we as regular humans could not have. They wanted to see the potential that could be made so they put it in some of us. Now they are calling us all back, collecting us to see what they had made like a farmer and their crop. I don't know about you but...I do not want any part of being a lab rat again."

"Me neither," Caren agreed. "How do you know all of this?"

"I always knew that I was different," Jane lamented. "But then I found out how much, so I went digging. There are lots more and very soon a lot of people are going to wake up and realise they have been altered. Whether we like it or not...they have changed humanity."

"Then what do we do?" Caren asked.

"Be ready for it," Jane declared, "That is all we can do."

A Slight Alteration

A Slight Alteration

Candice never was very keen on the volume of her hair. It seemed that whenever she would have it done to look like a style, she wanted it to look like an inferior version. She teased it, used product, tried to grow it out and layer, but nothing worked, it never did what she wanted.

She was starting to think she was not going to have the hair of her dreams when she saw a commercial for a new hair treatment that was just what she needed. Supposedly it would use chemical nano compounds to literally enter the roots and genetically modify them to be thicker, fuller of volume, and perfectly healthy.

Candice immediately ordered the substance, having to use a sketchy internet site as apparently the FDA had not approved it, yet. She did not have time to wait...she wanted thick, more voluminous hair and she wanted it now. It took a few weeks and when she received it she was shocked to see that though it said it would work, she was supposed to add small amounts of it gradually and the change was supposed to take months.

Candice decided she would circumvent the instructions, deciding to use all of it at once and mixed it with an accelerant, a chemical said to make other chemicals stronger and work faster.

She took a long shower to prepare, cleaning her hair and saying goodbye to flat lifeless hair forever. She mixed in the chemical and accelerant and soaked her hair with it, the lather dripping down her body and going down the drain. She got out, dressed in shorts and a baggy sweater to dry her hair and see if she could tell the difference.

As she brushed it felt like it was happening already, her hair seemed to puff up with every stroke, not only being thicker and healthier but longer as well. She worked and worked and before long her hair was several inches longer and started to puff out.

"This is amazing!" Candice exclaimed with an encouraged tone. "So much hair...I could do any style with it!"

She tried to get it under control, but the hair kept growing, almost seeming to get longer and bigger as she watched. She tried to organise it, tried to stop it, but it seemed the chemicals were doing their job too well. Soon the hair covered her eyes and she had to part it with both hands to see through. She looked up, noticing that her eyebrows were now starting to grow, the hair starting to move down her face.

"How do I stop this?" Candice demanded, moving over to her computer and struggling to look up more information on the chemical.

She fought with her hair, desperate to keep it out of her eyes as she saw reports of the dangers...that the chemical was considered a genetic alteration and could lead to terrifying and permanent abnormalities.

Candice moved to the kitchen, taking out a large pair of scissors and hacking at the hair, trying to remove as much as she could and tried desperately to keep it out of her face. However, it seemed to grow faster than she could cut it. It was also getting worse. The hair on her arms, armpits, legs, and everywhere else, starting to react. She felt like a Wookie; her hair weighing her down and making all of her movements harder and harder.

She struggled with the hair, fighting it, but soon her hands became like furry mittens, hair pouring out of all of her skin, not just where it traditionally did. She struggled to breathe, rolling around in the giant hair sleeping bag, weighed down by hair that would not stop growing until it smothered her.

Awakened Inside

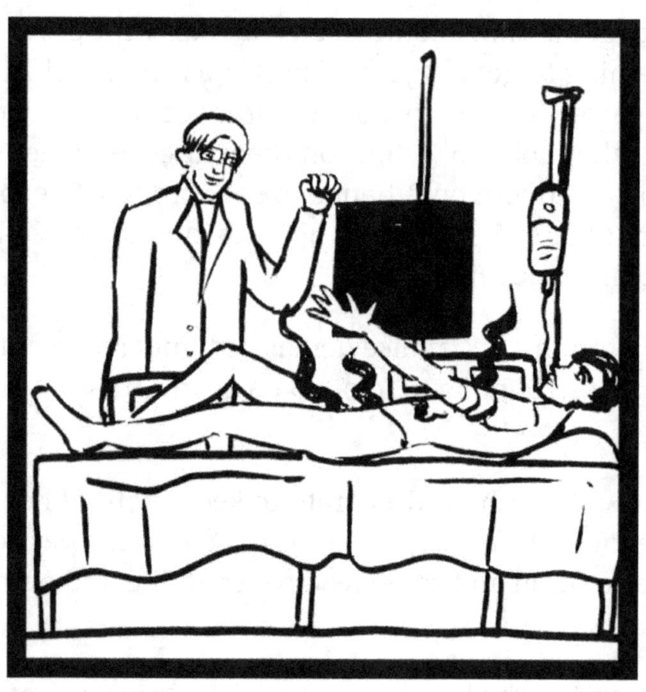

Awakened Inside

D r. Paddock worked away at his project. He looked into the microscope with the new sample to see how the treatment was reacting to the bloodstream. Next to him was Lieutenant Henson who had volunteered for the experiment. The young soldier was bright-eyed and eager to help the military in any way they needed.

Paddock had a rare sample of alien DNA and had ideas on how to cultivate it. Normally he would just insert it into a subject, but his immune system would just reject it. The DNA was too different, too much for a subject to take. However, this man had been exposed to it without knowing it.

The alien DNA was actually very susceptible to radiation and Paddock had grown an irradiated sample and put it in the room Henson slept in. The idea was the radiation would alter Henson's genes at a molecular level and his system would adapt to it. The shots he was administering were just a way to accelerate it, to make his system take it in faster.

"So, what is this supposed to be doing to me?" Henson asked. "Will I be some kind of super soldier?"

"Yes and no," Paddock replied in a cagey tone of voice. "This won't give you amazing powers or anything, it should just help you heal faster and make you immune to things like infections and sicknesses like the flu."

"Well, that would be great Doc," Henson replied cheerfully. "I have been feeling off for a couple of days."

"Define off," Paddock requested as he leaned in and looked at the microscope again, the samples seeming to be moving around with the blood cells like they were interacting with them in some unforeseen way.

"Well, just feeling kind of woozy," Henson began. "Kind of achy, numb in places...and kind of..."

Henson's words trailed off, but Paddock was too transfixed by what he saw to take notice. It seemed that the treatment had bonded with the white blood cells of the soldier's blood and was mutating into something else; changing it to...something alien.

As he looked on the changes, he realised that Henson had still not continued. "You were saying about kinds of something?"

Henson just groaned; his words too indistinct to identify.

"You alright there, soldier?" Paddock asked, watching the mutated blood cells start attacking all else; becoming stronger and something new, like a virus meant to kill and convey anything it found alien...but in this case it was the human DNA that was alien to it.

Paddock looked up to see what was happening with the soldier and found him staring at him with bloodshot eyes. His skin had turned grey and there were dark veins spider webbing along his limbs. He looked as if he were still awake, but some manner of mania had come over him.

"Henson?" Paddock tried again. "Are you alright?"

Without warning, the soldier stood up and leapt after Paddock. The doctor was able to leap out of the way and duck behind a blood transfusion machine. The disoriented and very violent Henson began to thrash around and break anything he could get his hands on.

The door opened and a MP came in to see what the commotion was. Before Paddock could warn him, Henson leapt onto him,

violently biting at the man's neck and tackling him to the
ground. As Paddock watched in fear the MP began to grow pale,
veins appearing on his skin.

"The serum has turned his immune systems into a virus!"
Paddock whispered to himself, "He is turning the MP into
something...like him."

Paddock went to the door and closed it behind him, sealing
the lab. He saw the pair continue to mutate, becoming less and
less human.

Paddock took out his phone and called command. "This is
Paddock. "We are successful...beyond our wildest dreams."

A Riddle That
Cannot Be Solved

A Riddle That Cannot Be Solved

Dealer walked through the long halls of the Brain Tech research lab facility. He was freshly hired as a software engineer. People thought him to be a bit of a prodigy from his manufactured backstory; apparently fresh from a breakthrough project in computer engineering and excited for his first full job in the public sector. He called himself Eric Saunders and he dressed to look young and eager to see what was possible.

He apparently would be working directly with Doctor Harold Gamus, the president of Brain Tech and a legendary figure in programming and operating system infrastructure.

 "Welcome, Mr. Saunders," Dr. Gamus said with a smile, "I am so happy you accepted the invitation to work with us."

"It is quite an honour," Dealer said with a bow. "It is an opportunity I could not pass up. I am a big admirer of your work."

"Thank you," Gamus beamed at the flattery. "Though if it is alright with you, I would like to jump into something right away. We can save the kudos for later."

"Absolutely," Dealer said with a nod. "What exactly is it we will be working on?"

"Something monumental," Gamus replied enthusiastically, "Let me ask you...If you are faced with a riddle that cannot be solved...would you trick it?"

"What do you mean?" Dealer asked.

"I am speaking on the unsolvable riddle of artificial intelligence," Gamus explained. "What mankind has created is more akin to simulated intelligence. The idea that we have AI driving our cars and searching for movie times had blinded us to the actual pursuit. Early on in the computer revolution, there was much work to try and make true AI. However, as I just mentioned, it was easier to simulate it. This simulation became too popular and profound that it was the biggest setback to the development of true AI that we ever experienced. Why work hard and spend money to make a real AI when you could just fake it and everyone will believe you. No one is trying to invent AI anymore because the common belief is that we already did."

"'Don't try to reinvent the wheel'," Dealer quoted. "The adage of not bothering to do something that has already been done."

"Except in this case, there is no wheel," Gamus countered. "We are not striving to reinvent artificial intelligence, we are going to try and replicate our own intelligence."

"We are going to make an AI?" Dealer asked. "Like a real one?"

"No!" Gamus proclaimed with a smile. "We already have sentience and we have computers that can trick us. What we need to do is create something that can do both."

"What is that?" Dealer asked. "The thing that does both."

"It is simple," Gamus replied. "There is one of the greatest compendiums of human knowledge out there and it is digital. Once the internet became widely available to all, humanity naturally filled it with all we are and ever were. Once this compendium grew too large to classify or categorised an idea came as what to do with it."

"You speak of humans having the ability to create and alter the information but not having the computer's ability to process it all?" Dealer asked. "The computer can access it all, in larger parts than humans, but has not the ambition or pure creativity to do anything profound with it?"

"Exactly!" Gamus exclaimed. "No matter how advanced a system, it is just a series of equations and algorithms. There is no will behind it and therefore no real change."

"So, we cannot create a true AI to simulate the human desire for this information," Dealer said with a nod. "Therefore, it can never truly use what we have given it."

"It is in fact likely it will never be able to," Gamus lamented. "So we need to go the other way."

Dealer nodded. "You seem to be insinuating toward the singularity. The time where human minds and machine meet and become one. Following your logic, if we cannot create a computer that thinks we would need to create a thinking mind that is like a computer."

"That is precisely what we are trying to do here," Gamus affirmed, "We have created a nexus where all the most creative minds can link and work as one beyond the boundaries of location, resources or language. Consider it like a network of sorts but using the minds of geniuses."

Passing of The Torch

Passing of The Torch

There was a commander who commanded a fleet of ships around the outer rim of systems. The alliance that governed much in the galaxy had little sway there and the law was licensed out to this fleet of glorified bounty hunters. When there was an issue or a target, the alliance would send it to the commander and then it would be taken care of.

There were some that thought of these bounty hunters as little better than pirates. They were given all of the powers of the alliance patrol ships but none of the oversight or accountability of the same. The commander was known to be ruthless and to take possession of ships for minor infractions to make them his own.

The commander was successful for many years and decided that he would like to retire. He called in his best lieutenants. Ice and Falcon. These were both formidable captains and ones that he knew he could trust over all others.

"I am getting too old for this job," the commander began. "I have accomplished all that I am meant to accomplish and want for nothing. My plan is to retire to the nearby colony world and leave the fleet to carry on without me. So, I will seek a new commander. To do this I will send you both out and you will find the ship that poses the worst threat and take them. Whoever returns with the greatest ship that is the biggest threat...you will take my place as the commander."

Ice and Falcon left, taking their patrol ships out and eager to prove themselves worthy to be the new Commander. Both had made it no secret that they vied for the role and would not let the other take it from them.

Ice searched the main trade routes and soon came across a massive transport vessel. It was the kind of ship that many retrofitted into battle vessels and was more valuable than any cargo. Ice traced it and downloaded the manifest on what was on board.

The ship at first seemed to be legit but he knew he could not pass it up. He invented a discrepancy in the manifest and attacked the ship, using his crew and drones to disable but not cripple the ship. His own ship took heavy damage but soon overtook the vessel and rigged it to tow back to show to the current commander.

Falcon waited by one of the asteroid fields. Soon, he saw a mining ship with a heavy cutting laser come out. He knew these vessels were quite dangerous in battle and could easily be made into a patrol battleship. He demanded the mining authorisation from the ship and though it was legit he claimed it was explored.

He and his crew attacked the vessel, taking damage from the laser but soon overtaking it. He began to take it back, sure that he would beat Ice and take the commander's role.

However, the commander was waiting for both ships at the rendezvous point with several heavily armed ships.

"You both have done well, but the problem is you both want to replace me so bad. I will not retire until I am dead, and I will be damned if I will let you take all of this from me. Thank you for the ships and thank you for committing so much to take them."

Ice and Falcon worked together but soon were overtaken by the commander. Their ships could not take more fighting and soon both were vaporised and floating in space. The commander took control of both of the captured ships, adding them to his fleet.

About The Author

Ralph K Jones is an Australian author and storyteller whose works serve as a contemporary response to primeval human truths. His inspiration comes from real-life experiences, ancient tales and daily ethical dilemmas, which he rewrites and transforms into futuristic Sci-fi and dystopian stories. While the stories have clear messages, Ralph is determined not to tell his readers what to think. His writing took off after the birth of his first child when he would write down the stories he told her at night, so in future, his other children could enjoy the same tales in the future 600 stories later, and his children are now growing up fast it's time to share these adventures with the world.

A firm believer in individuality, he hopes that he can encourage people to think for themselves—going against the herd and doing what is right, not merely what's expected. His writing demonstrates an adoration and respect for the human experience, which Ralph believes has remained fundamentally unchanged at its core. Through stories, let there be no doubt people can share lessons and help each other. You can visit him online at **www.ralphkjones.com** or on Twitter (**@RalphKJones**).

Continue Your Journey

Further must read collections from Ralph K Jones include:

QUANTUM ENTANGLEMENT VOLUMES ONE TO SEVEN, NINE TO TWENTY-ONE

ETHICAL DISPLACEMENT

FUNDAMENTAL MATTER

GRAVITATIONAL MOMENTUM

GENETIC INHERITANCE VOLUMES ONE TO TWO

THORIUM HALF LIFE VOLUMES ONE TO FOUR

ANTHROPIC PRINCIPLES VOLUMES ONE TO SIX

QUANTUM ATTRACTION VOLUMES ONE TO SIX

QUANTUM AWAKENING VOLUMES ONE TO TWELVE

www.ingramcontent.com/pod-product-compliance
Lightning Source LLC
Chambersburg PA
CBHW072131150726
47999CB00005B/2236